# Arabian Nights
# The Fisherman and the Genie

Indrani Vohra

Om KIDZ
An imprint of Om Books International

Once upon a time there lived a fisherman with his wife and three children. He used to throw his fishing nets out in the sea every day. One day, he threw out the net only to find that he had caught a donkey. Surprised by this catch, he prayed to God for forgiveness as he thought this was the result of his sins. He threw his net a second time and caught a pitcher full of broken glass and mud. Once again he prayed to God for forgiveness.

When he threw the net for the third time, it brought back a golden jar covered with a lid. He knelt upon the sand and studied the jar. He stuck a finger inside but felt nothing. He turned it upside down but nothing fell out. Just as he was about to toss the jar back into the sea, a thick cloud of smoke formed and out came a genie!

The fisherman was in awe. 'Genie, how did you come to be shut inside this jar?' asked the fisherman.

'I shall grant you one thing,' the genie said, without answering his question. 'You may choose your manner of death.'

'Why would you kill me?' the fisherman asked in fright.

'Hear my story and you shall understand,' replied the genie.

'It began long ago, when I rebelled against the King of the Genies. To punish me, the king enclosed me in this jar and sealed it with a lid. That should have been bad enough, but then he flung the jar into the sea. For the first century of my captivity, I swore to honour the man who would release me with many riches. A century passed but no one rescued me.'

‘During the second century of my captivity, I vowed to give all the treasures in the world to the man who would set me free. Another hundred years passed but no one came. In the third century, I swore I would make my saviour the king of the world, staying near him at all times, granting him three wishes each day.

But another century passed and I was still trapped in the jar. Filled with hopelessness, my anger grew so great that at last I vowed that whoever set me free would be punished with death; his only wish to be granted would be to choose the manner of his death. So you must choose,' the genie explained.

The fisherman understood that he needed to use his wits to get out of the situation, so he devised a plan. He said to the genie, 'Tell me genie, did you really live inside this small jar? It's hard to believe that this jar could contain even the smallest portion of someone as massive as you. I won't believe such a thing. It is impossible,' declared the fisherman.

‘How dare you?’ cried the genie out of anger. He began to transform again into smoke. He twisted himself into a spinning mass, tighter with every passing second and slid back into the jar. ‘There!’ he bellowed from inside, his voice echoing. ‘Do you believe me now?’

The fisherman quickly put the cap on the jug and said, 'Now I shall toss you back into the sea and I will leave a warning to all fishermen who cast their nets here-never open a golden jar you find in these waters.'

‘You tricked me!’ the genie cried. ‘Take off the lid. I promise not to harm you. I will repay you with tremendous wealth.’

The fisherman shook his head and said, ‘I cannot trust you,’ and tossed the jar into the sea where, people say, it still remains to this day.